For my daddy, who never complained about missing out on fishing,
and for John: daddy extraordinaire. —L. E.

Thanks to my dad, who taught me to move mountains with a smile,
and for the secret ingredient of his tomato sauce. —E. F.

STERLING CHILDREN'S BOOKS
New York

An Imprint of Sterling Publishing Co., Inc.
1166 Avenue of the Americas
New York, NY 10036

Text © 2018 Lezlie Evans
Cover and interior illustrations © 2018 Elisa Ferro

ISBN 978-1-4549-2171-4

Distributed in Canada by Sterling Publishing Co., Inc.
c/o Canadian Manda Group, 664 Annette Street
Toronto, Ontario M6S 2C8, Canada
Distributed in the United Kingdom by GMC Distribution Services
Castle Place, 166 High Street, Lewes, East Sussex BN7 1XU, England
Distributed in Australia by NewSouth Books
45 Beach Street, Coogee NSW 2034, Australia

For information about custom editions, special sales, and premium and corporate purchases,
please contact Sterling Special Sales at 800-805-5489 or specialsales@sterlingpublishing.com.

Manufactured in China

Lot #:
2 4 6 8 10 9 7 5 3 1
02/18

sterlingpublishing.com

The artwork for this book was created using gouache, colored pencil, and ink.
Cover and interior design by Heather Kelly

DADDIES DO

by
LEZLIE EVANS

illustrated by
ELISA FERRO

STERLING CHILDREN'S BOOKS
New York

Who tangles and wrangles
and wrestles for fun,
then cries, "I surrender!
You're tougher. You won!"?

Who takes you on outings
and simply won't care
if you've picked your own outfit
or have messy hair?

DADDIES DO.
THAT'S WHO!

Who makes you feel big
even though you are small?
Who asks you to stand
with your back to the wall—
then measuring tells you,
"You're growing so tall"?

DADDIES DO.
THAT'S WHO.

APRIL

MARCH

FEBRUARY
JANUARY

Who offers you courage
to give it a try,
then says you did great
even when you don't fly?

Who lets you help out?
Who works by your side,
and if you mess up
says, "I'm glad that you tried"?

DADDIES DO.
THAT'S WHO.

Who sits in the front row
when you're in a play
and takes lots of pictures
on your special day?

Who claps and barks loudest
when you've had your say?

DADDIES DO.
THAT'S WHO.

Who helps pass the time
when you're feeling sick?
Who cheers you right up
by doing a trick?

Who lifts you way up
to the top of the tree
because you're too short
and you'd like to see?

DADDIES DO.
THAT'S WHO.

Who knows what to fix
when you're craving a snack?
Who knows the best thing
for your hunger attack?
Who adds extra whipped cream,
then shares the tall stack?

DADDIES DO.
THAT'S WHO.

Who listens, who cares
when you've had a bad day?
Then in one fell swoop
helps your blues fly away?

Who builds the best forts,
and then glides down the slide?
Who catches you
after your slippery ride?

DADDIES DO.
THAT'S WHO.

Who takes you along
to the best fishing spot,
then patiently gets out
each tangle and knot?
Who lets you show off
all the fish that he caught?

DADDIES DO.
THAT'S WHO.

Who makes silly hairdos
when you're in the tub,
then blows giant bubbles
and helps you to scrub?

Who monkeys around—
lets you jump on the bed?
Then kisses you better
when you bump your head?

DADDIES DO.
THAT'S WHO.

Who reads the best stories
and snuggles with you,
then drifts off to sleep
before he is through?

Who gives you a bear hug
and tucks you in tight?
Who whispers, "I love you,"
then turns out the light?

GUESS WHO?
GUESS WHO?

DADDIES DO!